Merry Christmas, Stinky Face

Written by Lisa McCourt

Illustrated by Cyd Moore

Troll

BridgeWater Books

For that tiny creature who's already getting so many big~brother kisses through my belly button!
~ L.M.

For Lisa, whose words always inspire happy images and many smiles!
~ C.M.

Text copyright © 2002 by Lisa McCourt.

Illustrations copyright © 2002 by Cyd Moore.

Published by BridgeWater Books, an imprint and registered trademark of Troll Communications L.L.C.

Produced by Boingo Books, Inc.

Printed in China.

10 9 8 7 6 5 4 3 2 1

Library of Congress Cataloging-in-Publication Data

McCourt, Lisa.
    Merry Christmas, Stinky Face / by Lisa McCourt ; illustrated by Cyd Moore.
        p.   cm.
    Summary: As Christmas draws near, a young child is filled with questions abo
all of the things that could possibly go wrong, but Mama always finds a solutior
    ISBN 0-8167-7468-4
    [I. Christmas—Fiction. 2. Mother and child—Fiction. 3. Questions and answers—Fiction.] I. Moore, Cyd, ill. II. Title.

PZ7.M47841445 Me 2002
[E]—dc21   2002019035

Christmas was almost here. But I had a question.

Mama, what if the snow kept falling and falling so much that we couldn't open our door?

"I know what we'd do.
We'd crawl out of our window
into the snow with some cups
and juice. We'd sit in front
of our door and have a giant
snow-cone party until we'd
eaten up all the snow!"

But, Mama, what if we finally opened the door~ but then a big, wintry wind blew our Christmas tree away?

"If a wind did that, I would grab the coat rack from the hallway and decorate it with our brightest lights and ornaments. I'd put a star on the top, and we'd have a beautiful Christmas coat rack to sing our carols around."

red-nosed reindeer.

shiny hose...

But, Mama, but, Mama, what if I built a little snowman, and he followed me inside ... but our house was too warm and he started to **Melt?**

"It sounds like we'd have to set up a nice chilly room for him in the freezer. We'd give him peppermint ice cream for dinner and cover him with a blanket made of woven icicles so he'd stay frosty-cold all night long."

But, Mama, what if we were putting lights on our house, but we couldn't reach high enough?

And what if a giant Christmasaurus saw us and came to help?

"Well, of course, if a Christmasaurus helped, we'd have to thank her with some Christmas cookies and hot cocoa."

Okay, Mama. But what if Santa landed on our roof, and one of his reindeer got his antlers stuck in the branches of the tree that hangs over my bedroom window?

"Oh, that would be a problem, wouldn't it? Maybe we should leave your saw here in case Santa needs it to cut any branches."

But, Mama, but, Mama, what if Santa's boot falls off while he's driving the sleigh,

and his foot is so cold that he tries to wear my stocking on his foot ... but it doesn't fit?

"Hmmm. I guess we could leave these warm snow boots out with the saw— just in case."

What if the sleigh needs a new coat of paint?

What if the sack of toys starts to rip?

What if the reindeer need their fur brushed?

"There! That should do it."

Merry Christmas, Mama!

"Merry Christmas, my Stinky Face."